Dachshund Days

Meet the Gang

Bella

Sammy

Riley

Gracie

© 2019 Liz Gold Somekh and Stacey Maslin

Publisher: Playground Press

New York, NY

Website: www.dachshunddays.com

Illustrations: Maryann Held

ISBN 978-0-578-50371-4

Ave Clyde

Their story begins in a town called Biloxi,
when a friendship is formed by four little doxies.

They live in two houses that are side by side,
on a tree-lined street called Avenue Clyde.

Sammy and Riley
live at number four,
while Bella and
Gracie live right
next door.

One house is red
and the other is blue,
with a fence in the
middle separating
the two.

One day Sammy hears an unusual sound.
He thinks it is Riley just fooling around.

SQUEAK, SQUEAK is the sound
he hears coming from toys.
"Oh my, Riley, please,
stop making that noise!"

"It isn't me," she says, "let's go look outside."
"I won't go," Sammy says, and runs in to hide.

Sammy is scared and hides under the bed, but Riley loves fun and just runs ahead.

She calls out to Sammy,
"Come out and explore.
There are two other doxies
in the backyard next door."

But the fence in the middle
is blocking the way.
"YIKES," Riley cries,
"we just want to play!"

So Riley the rascal runs over to dig,
and under she creeps through a hole so big.

"Sammy, follow me, I got through!" she shouts.
Sammy can't resist and slowly comes out.

As Gracie looks up, she is jumping for joy.
"New friends to play with, one girl and one boy!"

As they all reach the fence,
there's a BIG surprise.
They can hardly believe what's
in front of their eyes.

The four dogs look just like each other!

"How could this be,
that she looks like me,
and the other looks
just like my brother?"

Gracie grabs Riley and they begin to run.
"HOORAY!" Riley cries, "let's go have some fun."

Bella picks up a ball and throws it so far.

Sammy jumps up to catch it.
He's a true baseball star!

As they head to the toys they see scattered around,
Riley spots a huge slide and cries, "Look what I found!"

"But someone is missing.
Where did Bella go?
She was chasing a squirrel
just a minute ago!"

They turn to find Bella
and suddenly see,
she has followed a squirrel
and bumped into a tree!

And quick as a flash,
Bella is on her way.
"I'm coming, I'm coming,
I'm ready to play!"

Gracie calls out to Bella
because Bella is blind.
"Hurry up, come join us,
don't get left behind!"

They all join in and go on the swings,
jump rope, play games, and
do lots of fun things.

They climb up the steps
to go down the slide.
"*Whee!*" Gracie cries.
"That was such a fun ride."

Wheee!

"Sammy, slide down,
it's not that high."
"I'm scared," Sammy says.
"I don't want to try."

"C'mon," Bella says,
"I will go down with you.
Just hold onto me,
we can do this too."

SWISH they go down and Sammy
shouts out with glee.
"Thanks, Bella," he says,
"for coming with me."

They hear a loud yawn and all turn their heads.
Riley shouts out, "I'm tired, I must go to bed!"

Exhausted, they all fall asleep right away,
each dreaming about their incredible day.